Prayers for gmings

Sammy Cross

Published by Sammy Cross, 2024.

This is a work of fiction. Similarities to real people, places, or events are entirely coincidental.

PRAYERS FOR NEW BEGINNINGS

First edition. October 28, 2024.

Copyright © 2024 Sammy Cross.

ISBN: 979-8224579419

Written by Sammy Cross.

Prayers for New Beginnings

Prayers for starting fresh, whether it's a new year, a new job, or a new chapter in life.

We all encounter moments in life when the horizon beckons us to start afresh, whether it's embarking on a new career, moving to a new city, or embracing a new year. These transitions can be exhilarating yet intimidating, full of promise but also tinged with uncertainty. Prayers for New Beginnings is a companion for these times, offering words of hope, encouragement, and guidance as we step into unknown chapters.

In this book, each prayer is crafted to nurture the spirit, to bolster courage, and to invite divine presence into the process of starting anew. Here, you'll find prayers for every kind of beginning — prayers for courage, clarity, patience, and forgiveness; prayers that invite us to let go of what no longer serves and embrace what lies ahead with open hearts and minds. Together, they create a tapestry of blessings, reminders that each new chapter is a gift, a chance to rewrite our narratives with the wisdom we've gained along the way.

The journey of new beginnings is sacred and deeply personal, yet universal in its challenges and opportunities. These prayers are not simply words but invitations to connect with the divine, to seek guidance and strength from a higher source as we set our intentions and pursue our hopes.

Whether you're stepping into a new season with excitement or trepidation, these prayers are here to walk alongside you, helping to ground you in faith and bring peace and assurance to the journey. May they serve as gentle reminders that you are never alone on this path, that every beginning holds the potential for growth, joy, and fulfilment.

So take a deep breath, open your heart, and let's begin this journey together.

Prayer for Courage to Start Anew

Prayer for Courage to Start Anew
    Dear God, I come with trembling heart,
    To find the strength for a brand new start.
    Give me courage, fierce and true,
    To walk with faith in all I do.
    Help me face each change with grace,
    To stand tall in this unknown place.
    Release my fears, let doubts subside,
    With You as my unfailing guide.
    In Your presence, fear departs,
    Fill my soul, calm my heart.
    May courage rise and doubts be few,
    As I embrace the journey new.
    Hold my hand, as I step in light,
    Through every shadow, dark or bright.
    With trust in You, I cannot fall,
    My courage lies in You, my all.

Prayer for Wisdom and Guidance

Lord, guide my steps, lead the way,
With wisdom clear for each new day.
When paths are blurred and vision dim,
Let me hear Your voice within.
Show me where to place my feet,
When faced with choices, incomplete.
Grant me eyes to see what's true,
To walk the path You've called me to.
In every twist, in every turn,
May I seek and humbly learn.
Lead me on with gentle hand,
To Your wisdom, true and grand.
I trust Your plans, Your perfect way,
Through each dawn, night, and day.
Guide me, Lord, forever near,
Your voice, my light, dispelling fear.

Prayer for Letting Go of the Past

Lord, I release the weight I bear,
The hurts, regrets, and silent prayer.
Help me lay my burdens down,
To wear instead Your peace's crown.
Unclench my hands, set my spirit free,
From past's grip, unbinding me.
Teach me, Lord, to leave behind,
All that binds my heart and mind.
Through pain and loss, I seek release,
In Your love, I find my peace.
With gentle strength, You bid me go,
To rise again and freely grow.
As I journey into new terrain,
Let past's shadows not remain.
With open heart, I'm ready now,
To live anew, and to You, I bow.

Prayer for Patience in New Beginnings

Lord, grant me patience to abide,
Through every high and every tide.
In each delay, in waiting's strain,
Teach me trust and peace to gain.
Help me rest when days are slow,
To trust in what I cannot know.
In moments quiet, still my soul,
Remind me, Lord, You're in control.
When time seems long and progress slow,
Give me strength to wait and grow.
With quiet heart, let patience bloom,
And chase away impatience's gloom.
I'll wait on You, O steady hand,
In faithfulness, Your promise stands.
With patience, I will journey on,
Until Your perfect work is done.

Prayer for Resilience in Trials

Lord, through trials, storms, and rain,
Let my spirit rise again.
Give me strength to stand upright,
Through darkest days and endless night.
When hardships press on every side,
Be my comfort, be my guide.
Let resilience be my song,
To face each trial, brave and strong.
With every fall, I rise anew,
Clothed in strength, made whole in You.
Through valleys deep and mountains steep,
Your promises, I'll surely keep.
No storm can shake this heart of mine,
For I am Yours, by Your design.
With steadfast hope, through loss and pain,
In You, my resilience will remain.

Prayer for Strength in the Unknown

God of might, my steady rock,
Hold me firm as I unlock
The doors to paths not yet revealed,
Give strength to face what is concealed.
In moments weak, when courage wanes,
Let Your power break my chains.
Grant me strength to persevere,
Through every doubt and every tear.
When the way is dark and steep,
Be the strength that I can keep.
Through storms that roar and winds that bend,
Stand with me, a faithful friend.
My strength, my hope, I find in Thee,
Through trials, Lord, stay close to me.

Prayer for Trust in Uncertain Times

Lord, help my heart to fully trust,
When earthly plans turn to dust.
In unknown fields where I must go,
Let trust in You bloom and grow.
Teach me, Lord, to walk by faith,
In every step, secure and safe.
Through each twist, each turn anew,
I place my confidence in You.
When questions rise and answers fade,
Let my trust in You be made.
For You alone, my path reveal,
In You, my trust is firm and real.
Lead me forth, both sure and true,
With heart that fully trusts in You.

Prayer for Peace in the Journey

Lord, bring peace to anxious mind,
Help me leave each fear behind.
When future days seem veiled and blurred,
Let Your peace be my assured.
Calm my thoughts, still my soul,
As You lead and take control.
In quiet trust, I'll find my way,
Through every night and every day.
May Your peace, like rivers flow,
In this path where I must go.
When storms arise and worries flare,
Be the peace that answers prayer.
In every step, both near and far,
Let peace be my guiding star.

Prayer for Inspiration in New Beginnings

God of creation, spark within,
A light where dreams and hope begin.
In new beginnings, inspire me,
To walk with courage, bold and free.
Let creativity abound,
In silent thought and joyful sound.
Guide my heart, my hands, my mind,
In each fresh vision I shall find.
When doubts arise, let courage grow,
With faith to push, to rise, to go.
Through new ideas, both deep and wide,
Be my light, my source, my guide.
In each endeavour, pure and bright,
Inspire me, Lord, with Your light.

Prayer for Strength in New Partnerships

Lord, bless this partnership with Your presence,
A relationship built on trust and mutual respect.
Help us to communicate openly and honestly,
To value each other's perspectives and strengths.
May we learn to work together with patience,
Uplifting and encouraging each other daily.
Let our partnership be grounded in integrity,
So that it reflects unity and shared purpose.
Guide us through challenges with resilience,
Helping us to find strength in collaboration.
In our shared goals and mutual respect,
May we honour each other and the path we walk.
Lord, may this partnership be a blessing to us,
And to all those we encounter along the way.

Prayer for Community and Connection

Lord, I thank You for this community around me,
For the opportunity to connect and belong.
Open my heart to those I meet along this path,
To find shared purpose and compassion in our journey.
Help me to give of myself in kindness and care,
To embrace those with different stories and views.
May I be a source of encouragement and light,
Helping to build bonds that uplift and strengthen.
Teach me to respect each individual's journey,
Celebrating diversity and unity in equal measure.
Let these connections grow in love and understanding,
Creating a space where all feel valued and seen.
Bless this community with peace and unity,
That we may reflect Your love in all we do.

Prayer for Romantic Relationships

Lord, bless this budding relationship with love,
Let trust and understanding be the foundation.
Guide us to be patient, gentle, and sincere,
To grow together in a spirit of mutual respect.
Help us to nurture each other's dreams and hopes,
To encourage and uplift one another daily.
May we face challenges with grace and resilience,
Learning to communicate openly and honestly.
Teach us to build this relationship on faith,
With hearts open to Your guidance and wisdom.
Let our love be a source of strength and joy,
A partnership that honours You in all ways.
Lord, may this relationship bring growth and blessing,
A journey of love, respect, and shared purpose.

Prayer for New Connections in Work and Purpose

Lord, thank You for the people I meet in my work,
For colleagues, mentors, and collaborators alike.
Help me to build connections rooted in respect,
That reflect integrity, trust, and shared purpose.
Grant me the wisdom to listen and learn,
To approach each person with openness and grace.
In every project and conversation,
May I reflect kindness, patience, and humility.
Teach me to value each connection, big or small,
As an opportunity to grow, serve, and uplift.
Let these relationships foster creativity and support,
That together, we may accomplish good work.
Lord, bless these connections with peace and unity,
And may they reflect the goodness of Your purpose.

Prayer for Growing Closer to Family

Lord, thank You for the gift of family,
For the relationships that shape who I am.
As I seek to grow closer to my loved ones,
Guide us all in love, patience, and understanding.
Help me to listen without judgment,
To honour each family member's unique journey.
Teach me to forgive easily and love fully,
To let go of past hurts and embrace new beginnings.
In times of tension, may I respond with grace,
And in moments of joy, may I celebrate fully.
Let these bonds be strengthened by compassion,
Nurtured by kindness and a willingness to grow.
Lord, bless our family with unity and peace,
A circle of love that reflects Your presence.

Prayer for Patience in New Endeavours

Prayer for Patience in Growth

Lord, grant me patience as I step forward,
Not rushing the process, but trusting in each moment.
Help me to see growth as a journey, not a race,
And to accept that every step has its purpose.
When I face setbacks and my progress feels slow,
Remind me that patience brings strength to endure.
Teach me to embrace each lesson fully,
Knowing that growth often comes in quiet, hidden ways.
Let me resist the urge to compare my path to others,
And instead, focus on the journey You have for me.
In times of delay, fill my heart with peace,
Assuring me that all things unfold in Your timing.
Guide me in wisdom to wait well,
To be steady and persistent, even when answers delay.
With patience as my companion, I trust in Your plan,
Moving forward one faithful step at a time.

Prayer for Patience Through Trials and Setbacks

Lord, as I encounter trials in this new path,
Grant me patience to face them without fear.
In moments of frustration and uncertainty,
Help me breathe deeply and trust in Your presence.
When setbacks arise and plans go astray,
May I find peace instead of impatience.
Let me see delays not as failures,
But as reminders that growth takes time.
Help me to rise again with calm resolve,
To embrace each challenge as part of the journey.
Teach me to respond with kindness toward myself,
And to trust that each setback carries a lesson.
With patience, may I persevere and stand firm,
Strengthened by the quiet assurance of Your guidance.
Lord, let this patience be a testament of faith,
And a reminder of Your hand at work in all things.

Prayer for Patience with Myself

Lord, grant me patience in the moments I struggle,
When I fall short or stumble along the way.
Help me to be gentle and forgiving with myself,
Trusting that progress often comes in small steps.
When I am tempted to criticize my efforts,
Remind me to celebrate each moment of growth.
Let me value the process, not just the outcome,
Seeing my journey as sacred and unique.
Teach me to accept my imperfections with grace,
And to know that each day brings new strength.
In moments of self-doubt, may patience be my friend,
Encouraging me to trust in the person I am becoming.
With every effort, let me be patient with myself,
Finding joy in each attempt, regardless of results.
Lord, guide me in love and understanding,
As I learn to walk this path with gentle patience.

Prayer for Patience in Uncertain Times

Lord, as I step into this new season,
Help me to embrace the uncertainties with patience.
Teach me to hold loosely to my own plans,
And to trust that Your timing is perfect.
When outcomes are unclear and answers are few,
May I find peace instead of anxiety.
Let me rest in the knowledge that growth takes time,
And that Your guidance will come in due season.
Grant me patience when the road seems long,
And courage to wait in faith and expectancy.
Remind me that the unknown is often where You work,
Bringing forth beauty in ways I cannot yet see.
With patience, I will walk this path each day,
Leaning not on my own understanding.
Guide me in calm assurance and steady peace,
As I place my trust in Your unfailing love.

Prayer for Patience with New Responsibilities

Lord, as I embrace new responsibilities,
Grant me the patience to handle them with care.
Help me to take on each task with diligence,
Without feeling overwhelmed or rushed.
When I feel stretched thin or uncertain,
Remind me to lean on You for strength and wisdom.
Let me approach each responsibility with peace,
Knowing that learning takes time and grace.
Teach me to prioritize what truly matters,
And to find joy in the tasks You've given me.
When my patience wears thin, renew my spirit,
Helping me to see the value in steady work.
With each new responsibility, may patience grow,
Rooted in trust and quiet determination.
Guide my hands and heart in all I do,
Filling me with calm patience for each day ahead.

Prayer for Clarity in Purpose

Lord, I come seeking clarity of purpose,
To understand the calling You have placed within me.
Help me to discern what truly matters,
And to let go of distractions that cloud my way.
Show me the gifts You've planted in my life,
And teach me to use them with intention and love.
May I pursue goals that honour Your purpose,
Choosing paths that bring joy, growth, and peace.
In moments of doubt, steady my heart,
And remind me of the vision You have for me.
Fill my mind with understanding and clarity,
That I may live each day with direction and grace.
With a clear sense of purpose, I walk forward,
Rooted in the plans You have prepared for me.

Prayer for Wisdom in Decisions

Lord, in this new season of choices,
I seek wisdom to make decisions aligned with You.
Give me clarity in seeing the bigger picture,
To understand how each choice shapes the journey.
When paths diverge and I feel uncertain,
Let Your light be the guide I rely on.
Help me to weigh each option thoughtfully,
With a heart that trusts Your wisdom above all.
Teach me patience to consider carefully,
And courage to move when the way is clear.
Let each decision I make reflect Your goodness,
And bring me closer to the purpose You intend.
With Your wisdom and vision, may I choose well,
Walking with clarity, faith, and discernment.

Prayer for Focus Amid Distractions

Lord, help me to stay focused in this new phase,
To seek Your clarity when distractions surround me.
Teach me to recognize what serves my purpose,
And to let go of what pulls me away from Your path.
Fill my mind with clarity of thought and intention,
So I may walk with purpose and commitment.
When I am tempted to stray from my goals,
Ground me in the vision You have placed in my heart.
Help me to prioritize with wisdom and grace,
Choosing what aligns with Your will for me.
Let me not be swayed by the noise of the world,
But stay centered in what truly matters.
With focus and clarity, may I fulfil Your purpose,
Each step anchored in Your guidance and love.

Prayer for Discernment in New Opportunities

Lord, as new opportunities unfold,
Grant me the vision to discern what is right.
Help me to see beyond the surface,
To recognize what aligns with Your plan for me.
Teach me to weigh each option with care,
Seeking clarity in both mind and spirit.
May I not be swayed by fleeting gains,
But look toward what holds lasting purpose.
Guide me in knowing when to move forward,
And when to let go, trusting in Your wisdom.
Fill me with peace in each decision I make,
Confident that You are guiding my choices.
With clarity, may I choose paths that honour You,
Each step aligned with Your purpose for my life.

Prayer for Clear Vision in Times of Doubt

Lord, when doubt clouds my way,
Grant me vision to see with clarity and faith.
Help me to look beyond my present worries,
And to remember the purpose You have for me.
When uncertainty pulls at my heart,
Let me lean on the vision You've planted within.
Teach me to see past the immediate struggle,
And to trust in the greater picture You hold.
Give me eyes to recognize Your hand at work,
Even when the path seems unclear or strange.
May I find peace in knowing You are guiding me,
With each step grounded in trust and purpose.
In moments of doubt, let vision remain,
Clear and true, a light guiding me onward.

Prayer for Self-Compassion and Acceptance

Prayer for Embracing My Whole Self

Lord, help me to see myself through Your eyes,
To embrace the person You created me to be.
Teach me to honour my strengths and my weaknesses,
Without judgment or harshness in my heart.
When I am tempted to criticize myself,
Remind me that I am made with love and care.
Let me see my imperfections as part of my journey,
Learning from them, not being defined by them.
Grant me kindness toward my own spirit,
And the grace to walk in peace with myself.
With Your love, may I find self-compassion,
Embracing all of who I am in this new beginning.

Prayer for Self-Compassion in Moments of Doubt

Lord, in times of self-doubt, draw me near,
Remind me to treat myself gently and kindly.
Help me to forgive myself for my mistakes,
To learn from them and let them go with peace.
May I recognize that growth is a journey,
And that every step, forward or back, has purpose.
Teach me to embrace my flaws with patience,
Knowing they are part of what makes me whole.
When I am hardest on myself, soften my heart,
Filling me with love and understanding.
With self-compassion, may I walk forward,
At peace with who I am and who I am becoming.

Prayer for Acceptance of My Imperfections

Lord, help me to accept myself completely,
Not only my strengths but my weaknesses, too.
Teach me that I am worthy of love and kindness,
Just as I am, even with my imperfections.
Let me release the need to be flawless,
And embrace the beauty of my humanity.
Grant me the courage to be vulnerable,
To show up in life as my true, whole self.
Guide me in treating myself with grace,
Remembering that I am a work in progress.
With Your love as my foundation,
May I accept myself fully and joyfully.

Prayer for Self-Compassion in Change

Lord, as I step into new beginnings,
Help me to be gentle with myself in the process.
When I stumble or feel unsure, grant me grace,
And remind me that change takes time.
Teach me to speak kindly to my own heart,
To treat my fears and insecurities with care.
Let me embrace the journey, imperfections and all,
Without pressure to have it all figured out.
May I find comfort in knowing I am enough,
Exactly as I am in this moment.
With compassion for myself, may I move forward,
Trusting in Your love to guide each step.

Prayer for Letting Go of Self-Judgment

Lord, free me from the chains of self-judgment,
Help me to release the harsh words I say to myself.
Teach me to replace criticism with kindness,
To see myself through the lens of compassion.
In moments when I fall short of my own expectations,
Let me forgive and embrace myself fully.
Guide me to recognize that I am growing,
And that perfection is not the goal You seek for me.
With every new beginning, may I find acceptance,
And the grace to start again without shame.
In Your love, let me find self-compassion,
Walking forward with a gentle heart.

Prayer for Favor in New Opportunities

Lord, as I embark on this new career,
I ask for Your favour in all that I do.
Help me to find doors that open with ease,
Guided by Your hand and led by Your grace.
Grant me connections that uplift and inspire,
And favour in the eyes of those I work with.
May my work be recognized and appreciated,
Reflecting the gifts You have placed in me.
Teach me to move forward with confidence,
Trusting that You will provide for my needs.
When challenges arise, may I face them bravely,
Knowing that You are with me always.
With Your favour upon me, may I thrive,
And find joy and purpose in this new path.

Prayer for Success and Fulfilment

Lord, in this new job, I seek Your blessing,
Asking for success that honours You.
Help me to set goals that align with Your will,
And to work with diligence and integrity.
Let my efforts bear fruitful outcomes,
That I may serve others with joy and commitment.
In each task, grant me focus and insight,
To learn and grow as I walk this path.
May I find fulfilment in the work I do,
Knowing that I am using my gifts purposefully.
Let my success bring glory to Your name,
And may I always remember to give thanks.
With gratitude and hope, I seek Your guidance,
Trusting in Your plan for my success.

Prayer for Peace in Career Transitions

Lord, as I transition into this new role,
Grant me peace amid the unknown.
Help me to let go of doubts and fears,
And to embrace this opportunity with faith.
In moments of uncertainty, be my calm,
Reassuring me that I am where I should be.
Teach me to adapt with patience and grace,
And to trust the process of learning anew.
May I find joy in discovering new skills,
And confidence as I grow in this position.
Let me see each challenge as a stepping stone,
And every success as a gift from You.
With peace in my heart, I walk this path,
Knowing that You are guiding every step.

Prayer for Purpose and Impact

Lord, as I begin this career path,
Help me to work with purpose and intention.
Let each day be an opportunity to serve,
Using my skills to make a positive impact.
May my work reflect Your love and kindness,
And be a source of encouragement to others.
Teach me to see my role as a calling,
Not just a job, but a way to bring goodness.
Guide me to tasks that benefit others,
And open my eyes to ways I can help.
Let my purpose be greater than myself,
Driven by compassion, faith, and humility.
In all I do, may I honour Your purpose,
Finding fulfilment in serving with love.

Prayer for Courage in Unfamiliar Paths

Lord, as I walk paths unfamiliar and new,
Grant me courage to move forward in faith.
When I feel hesitant or afraid of change,
Remind me that You are my steady guide.
Help me to welcome new opportunities,
And to let go of the comfort of the past.
Let me face each moment with a brave heart,
Believing that You equip me for what lies ahead.
Teach me to be bold in the face of uncertainty,
Finding strength not in what I know, but in You.
When doubts arise, calm my spirit with peace,
Reminding me that I am never alone.
With courage, may I embrace this season of change,
Open to the blessings that come with new beginnings.
Lord, let my strength in You be my foundation,
Guiding me with hope through all transitions.

Prayer for Resilience Through Challenges

Lord, in this season of shifting and change,
Grant me resilience to endure and grow.
Help me to adapt with grace and wisdom,
To bend without breaking, to rise above.
In moments of doubt or fatigue, renew me,
Remind me of the strength You have placed within.
May I face each day with determination and hope,
Finding joy in each step, even the hard ones.
Let resilience be my response to each obstacle,
A quiet resolve that fuels my perseverance.
Teach me to see setbacks as learning moments,
And to keep moving forward with faith intact.
Through every change, may I emerge stronger,
A testament to the power of resilience.
Lord, be my strength when my own feels weak,
And guide me with steady hands through this transition.

Prayer for Peace and Strength in Change

Lord, as I journey through this season of change,
Fill me with peace that transcends all fear.
Help me to find strength within, rooted in You,
A calm resolve to face whatever lies ahead.
In moments when change feels overwhelming,
Center me in Your peace, grounding my heart.
Let me be steady in the midst of uncertainty,
Finding comfort in Your unwavering presence.
May I approach each transition with openness,
Seeing it as a path to growth and new beginnings.
Guide me with wisdom, strengthen my resolve,
And remind me that peace is found in trusting You.
With peace and strength as my companions,
I walk forward, secure in Your love and grace.
Help me to embrace change, not with fear,
But with confidence in Your faithful guidance.

Prayer for Trust in the Unknown

Lord, as I step into unknown territory,
Grant me the strength to trust in Your plan.
Teach me to release the need for certainty,
And to find courage in simply trusting You.
Help me let go of what I cannot control,
Finding peace in surrender, not in worry.
When I am tempted to fear the unknown,
Remind me that You are already there.
May I have strength to embrace uncertainty,
With a heart open to new paths and blessings.
Let me trust that change is part of Your design,
A means to grow closer to You and to purpose.
In this season of change, be my foundation,
My constant, unshakable source of strength.
With trust in You, I face the unknown,
Knowing that Your love lights my way.

Prayer for Financial Wisdom

Lord, as I manage my resources each day,
Grant me wisdom in every decision I make.
Help me to be a faithful steward of what I have,
And to use it to serve others and honour You.
Teach me to prioritize what truly matters,
And to resist the lure of unnecessary gain.
Let my financial choices reflect integrity,
With a heart guided by gratitude and care.
May I trust in Your provision, not in excess,
And live with contentment in what You supply.
Guide me to be wise with my resources,
Using them to bless others and grow in grace.

Prayer for Abundance and Gratitude

Lord, I ask for abundance in this new season,
Not just in resources, but in joy and peace.
Help me to see each provision as a blessing,
To live each day with gratitude and contentment.
Teach me to use my abundance with purpose,
Sharing freely with those in need.
May my heart overflow with thankfulness,
And my hands be open to give as I receive.
Let abundance be a tool for generosity,
Not for storing up wealth, but for serving.
With a grateful heart, I welcome Your blessings,
Trusting in Your provision each day.

Prayer for Financial Peace

Lord, as I face financial needs and challenges,
Grant me peace and confidence in Your care.
Help me to trust that You see my needs,
And that You will provide in Your perfect timing.
Teach me to manage what I have faithfully,
And to be wise in planning for the future.
Let financial worries not cloud my heart,
But remind me that my worth is found in You.
May I seek peace in Your provision, not in wealth,
And find joy in living simply and purposefully.
With a calm spirit, I place my needs before You,
Knowing You are my provider and peace.

Prayer for Opportunities and Provision

Lord, I ask for opportunities to provide,
For doors to open in ways only You can give.
Grant me the chance to work and to grow,
To use my skills in meaningful ways.
Help me to seek out what aligns with purpose,
And to trust that You'll meet each need I have.
Let each opportunity bring not just wealth,
But fulfilment and joy in honest work.
Teach me to walk through doors You open,
And to trust Your timing in every opportunity.
With faith in Your provision, I move forward,
Knowing You will guide and sustain me.

Prayer for Generosity and Stewardship

Lord, as I receive blessings in this season,
Help me to be a good steward of all I have.
Teach me to live with open hands and heart,
Sharing freely, trusting in Your endless supply.
Let my resources be a tool for good,
Used wisely to serve and uplift others.
May I be generous with what You provide,
Not holding too tightly to wealth or gain.
Give me the wisdom to manage with care,
And the joy of giving back as You lead me.
With trust in Your abundance, I offer myself,
A steward of Your blessings in all I do.

Prayer for Open Doors and Opportunities

Prayer for Divine Guidance in Opportunities

Lord, I come with a heart open and willing,
Asking for Your guidance in new opportunities.
Show me the doors You wish to open,
And give me courage to step through them in faith.
Help me to recognize Your hand at work,
To discern the paths meant just for me.
Grant me wisdom to pursue what aligns with purpose,
And to let go of what is not in Your plan.
May I not fear the unknown, but trust in Your timing,
Believing You prepare a way even in the unseen.
Let each open door bring growth and blessing,
A chance to serve, learn, and draw closer to You.
With a grateful heart, I await Your guidance,
Ready to walk through doors You open before me.

Prayer for Courage to Embrace New Paths

Lord, as new doors open before me,
Grant me courage to step forward in trust.
Help me to see opportunity as a gift,
A path to grow and fulfil my calling.
Teach me to release fear of the unknown,
And to lean fully on Your steadfast presence.
Let my steps be guided by Your wisdom,
And my heart be open to all that awaits.
In every opportunity, may I honour You,
Serving with joy, humility, and purpose.
When doubts arise, remind me of Your faithfulness,
And fill me with strength to keep moving forward.
With each new door, may I grow in faith,
Embracing all that You have prepared for me.

Prayer for Patience in Waiting for Opportunities

Lord, as I wait for doors to open,
Grant me patience to trust in Your timing.
Help me to resist the urge to rush or force,
And to find peace in the stillness of waiting.
Teach me to prepare my heart and mind,
So I may be ready for what lies ahead.
Let me trust that You see the bigger picture,
And that each delay has purpose and grace.
May I find joy in the season of waiting,
Knowing You work even when paths are unseen.
With patience, I will wait with hope and faith,
Trusting You to open doors in Your perfect time.
In waiting, Lord, let my spirit be refined,
So I am ready for every opportunity You bring.

Prayer for Discernment in Choosing Paths

Lord, as opportunities unfold before me,
Grant me the discernment to choose wisely.
Help me to see with clarity and purpose,
To understand the doors meant just for me.
Teach me to listen to Your guidance,
And not be swayed by temporary desires.
Let me seek paths that align with Your will,
Not merely those that seem easy or quick.
May my choices reflect faith and integrity,
A willingness to walk in Your light and truth.
Guide me in recognizing true opportunity,
And give me strength to walk through each door.
With discernment as my guide, I move forward,
Trusting in Your wisdom above all else.

Prayer for Gratitude in Opportunities Given

Lord, for every door You have opened for me,
I offer thanks with a grateful heart.
Help me to see each opportunity as a blessing,
A chance to serve, grow, and learn in You.
Teach me to use what I am given wisely,
To honour You in all I pursue and create.
May I approach each task with humility,
Knowing that each door is a gift of grace.
When new paths appear, let gratitude lead me,
And remind me that You are my ultimate guide.
With a thankful spirit, I will walk forward,
Cherishing the ways You open before me.
In every door and every step, I give thanks,
For the abundant opportunities You provide.

Prayer for Healing from Fear and Anxiety

Lord, I ask for healing from the fears I carry,
The worries that shadow my steps forward.
Help me to find calm within the storm,
And peace to replace the burdens I bear.
Teach me to trust in Your constant presence,
To know that I am safe in Your hands.
Heal my anxious thoughts and heavy heart,
Releasing me from the grip of fear.
Let me face each day with renewed courage,
Freed from the anxieties of the past.
Guide me in trusting the path before me,
Knowing You walk beside me each step.
With Your healing touch, may I be restored,
Finding peace in both mind and spirit.

Prayer for Healing from Betrayal

Lord, I bring before You the hurt of betrayal,
The pain of broken trust and wounded heart.
Help me to process the hurt I feel,
And to seek healing beyond the scars.
Teach me to forgive, even when it's difficult,
And to release bitterness that holds me back.
May I find freedom from resentment's weight,
And the courage to trust once again.
Heal the parts of me that feel guarded,
And open my heart to love and hope anew.
Guide me in building healthy relationships,
Grounded in trust, kindness, and grace.
With Your healing, may I grow beyond this pain,
Embracing the promise of restored trust.

Prayer for Healing of the Inner Child

Lord, I ask for healing in the deepest parts,
The wounds I carry from years gone by.
Help me to nurture the child within,
To offer compassion where pain still lingers.
Teach me to embrace my younger self,
To see the hurt with understanding and love.
May I release the pain of past experiences,
And find joy in reclaiming my inner peace.
Heal the memories that still cause sadness,
And replace them with comfort and calm.
Guide me to wholeness in mind and spirit,
Embracing all of who I am and have been.
With Your love, may I restore what was lost,
And find peace in my heart's true healing.

Prayer for Strength in Overcoming Trauma

Lord, I ask for strength in this journey of healing,
For courage to face the trauma of my past.
Help me to confront the memories I fear,
And to find freedom on the other side of pain.
Teach me resilience in moments of struggle,
And patience as I walk this path of renewal.
May I feel Your presence with me always,
A reminder that I am never alone in this.
Heal the wounds that go unseen by others,
And restore the strength I thought was lost.
Guide me toward wholeness, step by step,
Finding light where there was once only shadow.
With Your grace, may I move forward in peace,
Restored and renewed in mind and heart.

Prayer for Self-Forgiveness and Healing

Lord, as I look back on my own mistakes,
Help me to embrace forgiveness for myself.
Teach me to see that I am more than my past,
And that I am worthy of grace and healing.
Release me from the guilt that weighs me down,
And help me to see myself through Your loving eyes.
May I learn to forgive my imperfections,
And find peace in the process of self-renewal.
Guide me to grow from my mistakes,
Not as chains, but as lessons in becoming whole.
Let my heart be free from the weight of shame,
Open to a future where I am kinder to myself.
With each act of self-forgiveness, renew me,
Reminding me that I am worthy of love and grace.
Lord, help me to forgive myself fully,
And walk forward in peace and acceptance.

Prayer for Renewal and Letting Go

Lord, I ask for the courage to let go,
To release the hurts and burdens of yesterday.
Help me to let go of old stories and wounds,
And to embrace the promise of renewal in You.
Teach me to forgive what has been done,
And to leave the past where it belongs.
May I find peace in letting go of bitterness,
And freedom in forgiving what once held me back.
With a heart open to fresh beginnings,
Guide me toward a future filled with hope.
Let forgiveness be the soil of my growth,
And renewal be the light that guides my way.
As I let go, may I find joy and freedom,
A life unburdened by anger or regret.
Lord, renew my spirit and heal my soul,
So I may live with a heart that forgives freely.

Prayer for Healing through Forgiveness

Lord, as I seek healing from past wounds,
Teach me the power of forgiveness.
Help me to see that forgiveness brings freedom,
That letting go is the key to peace.
May I forgive those who have caused me pain,
Releasing the hold of anger and resentment.
Show me how to free my heart from bitterness,
To walk lighter, unburdened by the past.
Teach me to forgive with compassion and grace,
Remembering that we all fall short at times.
Let forgiveness open my heart to love again,
And heal the scars that linger deep within.
With each act of forgiveness, may I find strength,
Renewed in the freedom that comes from letting go.
Lord, heal my heart and guide me forward,
With a spirit that chooses love over hurt.

Prayer for Renewal in Forgiveness

Lord, as I embrace forgiveness in my life,
Grant me the grace to renew my spirit.
Teach me to forgive without reservation,
To find strength in choosing peace over pain.
Help me to see forgiveness as an act of love,
A gift that I give to myself and others.
May I forgive not only those who've hurt me,
But also myself for the ways I've fallen short.
Guide me to live with a heart unburdened,
Free from the chains of anger and regret.
Let forgiveness renew my outlook on life,
Filling me with hope and gentle compassion.
With each act of forgiveness, may I grow,
A soul refreshed by grace and understanding.
Lord, lead me to embrace the power of renewal,
And to live with a heart that forgives fully.

Prayer for New Beginnings in Family Life

Prayer for Peace in Family Transitions

Lord, as we embark on this new chapter,
We ask for Your peace to fill our home.
Bless our family with harmony and love,
Guiding us gently through each transition.
Help us to support one another in grace,
To listen, understand, and uplift each other.
Teach us to face challenges with unity,
Strengthening our bonds in love and faith.
May our family be a place of comfort and joy,
A refuge filled with laughter, trust, and peace.
Guide us in each new step we take,
Letting Your wisdom shape our journey together.
With Your blessing, may we find peace in change,
And strength in the love we share as family.
Lord, be the foundation of our family's new beginning,
And let Your peace reign in every heart.

Prayer for Guidance in Marriage

Lord, as we enter this sacred covenant,
We ask for Your guidance in our marriage.
Teach us to love one another selflessly,
To honour and respect each other deeply.
Help us to build a foundation on trust,
Strengthened by patience, kindness, and grace.
Guide us through the joys and challenges,
With hearts that seek to grow together in You.
May our love be a reflection of Your love,
Pure, enduring, and filled with compassion.
Let our marriage be a source of joy and strength,
A partnership that thrives in unity and peace.
With Your guidance, may we cherish each other,
And build a life filled with laughter and hope.
Lord, bless this new beginning in our marriage,
And be the anchor of our journey together.

Prayer for New Beginnings in Parenthood

Lord, as we welcome this child into our lives,
We ask for Your blessing upon our family.
Teach us to nurture with patience and love,
To guide with wisdom and gentle care.
Help us to be the parents You call us to be,
Bringing up this child in kindness and grace.
May we show love in all that we do,
Creating a home that is safe and full of joy.
Grant us strength for the days and nights ahead,
And patience for the moments that test us.
Fill our hearts with gratitude and wonder,
As we embark on this beautiful journey of parenthood.
With Your blessing, may our family grow in love,
Enriched by the gift of this precious life.
Lord, guide us in this new beginning,
And be the foundation of our family's love.

Prayer for Strength in Family Growth

Lord, as our family grows and changes,
Grant us the strength to embrace each moment.
Help us to support one another fully,
To lift each other up with kindness and care.
Teach us to communicate with patience and love,
And to respect each person's journey and gifts.
Guide us through challenges with unity,
Keeping our hearts bound together in faith.
May our home be a sanctuary of peace,
Where each member feels valued and loved.
Give us the strength to face all transitions,
And to celebrate the joy that each brings.
With Your blessing, may our family be strong,
A testament of love, faith, and resilience.
Lord, walk with us in this new beginning,
And let Your grace lead us every day.

Prayer for Blessings in New Family Roles

Lord, as we step into new roles within our family,
Bless us with understanding and grace.
Help us to grow into these roles with joy,
And to embrace the changes they bring.
Teach us to be patient with one another,
To honour each person's strengths and dreams.
Guide us as we navigate unfamiliar paths,
Encouraging us to support one another deeply.
May our family be filled with laughter and love,
And may our home be a place of warmth and peace.
Let each new role strengthen our family bond,
And build a foundation of trust and faith.
With Your blessing, may we cherish these roles,
Finding joy in the love that binds us as family.
Lord, bless each of us in this new beginning,
And fill our home with Your endless peace.

Prayer for Creativity and Inspiration

Prayer for Fresh Inspiration

Lord, as I enter this new season,
I ask for a wellspring of fresh ideas.
Fill my mind with inspiration and vision,
Guide me in creating with purpose and joy.
Help me to see beauty in the ordinary,
And to find wonder in the simple things.
May my heart be open to new possibilities,
And my hands ready to bring them to life.
With Your guidance, let creativity flow freely,
A gift that reflects Your love and grace.
Lord, inspire me with a spirit of renewal,
And fill my days with creativity and light.

Prayer for Clarity in Creativity

Lord, as I create, grant me clarity of vision,
So that my ideas may flow with ease and purpose.
Help me to see clearly what I wish to express,
And to bring it to life with intention and grace.
Guide me in making choices that honour You,
Using my talents for good and for beauty.
Teach me to listen to the whispers of inspiration,
And to recognize Your hand in each idea.
May my creativity reflect truth and love,
A light that brings hope to those who see it.
Lord, grant me clarity in each project I begin,
And inspire me to create with heart and soul.

Prayer for Creativity in Every Day

Lord, fill my daily life with creativity,
A spark that lights up each moment with joy.
Help me to see creative potential in all things,
To find beauty in both big and small details.
Teach me to approach each day with wonder,
And to embrace the gift of creating anew.
May my thoughts be fresh, my ideas inspired,
A reflection of the beauty You place within me.
Let creativity be a natural part of my journey,
An expression of gratitude for Your gifts.
Lord, may I live each day with inspiration,
And bring creativity into all that I do.

Prayer for Joy in the Creative Process

Lord, as I create, fill me with joy,
The pure delight of bringing ideas to life.
Help me to cherish each step of the journey,
Finding meaning in both progress and pause.
Teach me to see creativity as a blessing,
A gift that mirrors Your boundless nature.
Let me approach my work with excitement,
Eager to see what each day brings forth.
May I find peace in the process itself,
And joy in every detail of what I create.
Lord, guide my hands and heart in creativity,
And let my work be a reflection of Your love.

Prayer for Healthy Boundaries

Prayer for Wisdom in Setting Boundaries

Lord, as I navigate new roles and relationships,
Grant me the wisdom to set healthy boundaries.
Help me to discern what I can give and receive,
And to recognize where limits are needed.
Teach me to honour my well-being and peace,
Without guilt or fear of disappointing others.
Let me be clear in my intentions and words,
Communicating my needs with honesty and grace.
Guide me to set boundaries rooted in love,
Both for myself and those around me.
May I find strength in saying "no" when needed,
And courage to protect what matters most.
With Your guidance, may my boundaries bring balance,
Preserving the peace You desire for me.
Lord, help me respect my own limits,
And build relationships that nurture my soul.

Prayer for Boundaries that Foster Peace

Lord, as I enter new situations and roles,
Help me to establish boundaries that protect my peace.
Teach me to value stillness and rest,
And to prioritize my mental and emotional well-being.
Guide me to create spaces of calm and safety,
Both within my heart and in my relationships.
Let me embrace boundaries as gifts of self-love,
Not walls, but paths to healthier connection.
May I feel peace in the choices I make,
Knowing they honour the life You've given me.
Help me to balance giving and receiving,
To nurture relationships without losing myself.
With Your guidance, may my boundaries bring calm,
A foundation for healthy, joyful living.
Lord, grant me the wisdom to protect my peace,
And to find comfort in the boundaries I keep.

Prayer for Healthy Boundaries at Work

Lord, as I step into new professional roles,
Guide me to establish boundaries that sustain me.
Help me to value my time and skills,
And to work with integrity without overextending.
Teach me to balance my duties with rest,
To recognize when it's time to pause and recharge.
May I set limits that prevent burnout,
And uphold a work-life balance that honours You.
Grant me the courage to communicate my needs,
With clarity, kindness, and self-respect.
Let me give my best without losing my peace,
Fulfilling my role while honouring my own health.
With Your blessing, may my work bring fulfilment,
Free from stress and strain beyond what's needed.
Lord, help me to find peace in healthy boundaries,
And to serve others while caring for myself.

Prayer for Boundaries that Reflect Self-Love

Lord, teach me that boundaries are acts of self-love,
Ways to honour the worth You've placed within me.
Help me to set limits that nurture my soul,
Guided by respect, care, and inner peace.
May I embrace boundaries without guilt or fear,
Trusting that they bring balance and well-being.
Let me release the pressure to please everyone,
And find comfort in protecting what's sacred to me.
Give me the courage to honour my needs,
And to build relationships that support my growth.
Teach me to communicate with honesty and love,
Creating space for mutual respect and care.
With Your wisdom, may my boundaries reflect love,
A testament to the value I hold in Your eyes.
Lord, help me live with confidence and grace,
Upholding boundaries that lead to a life of peace.

Prayer for Gratitude in the Present Moment

Prayer for Gratitude in Everyday Moments

Lord, help me to see the beauty in today,
To find joy in each simple, quiet moment.
Teach me to be grateful for small blessings,
And to cherish the gifts that surround me now.
May I see Your hand in the ordinary,
In every sunrise, every laugh, every breath.
Fill my heart with thankfulness for today,
For the life and love You've given me.
Help me to live fully in the present,
Without rushing toward what is yet to come.
With a spirit of gratitude, may I walk this path,
Embracing each step, each moment of grace.
Lord, let my heart overflow with gratitude,
For the countless blessings I receive each day.

Prayer for Gratitude and Contentment

Lord, cultivate within me a heart of contentment,
To find enough in what You have given today.
Help me to let go of striving and yearning,
And to rest gratefully in the present moment.
Teach me to appreciate what I have now,
Without longing endlessly for what lies ahead.
May I find joy in the gifts of this moment,
And let peace fill the spaces of my soul.
Guide me to live with a spirit of gratitude,
Thankful for the journey as it unfolds.
With contentment, may I walk in quiet joy,
Trusting that each day brings what I need.
Lord, let me be grateful for each breath,
Living each day as a blessing from You.

Prayer for Hope and Gratitude Together

Lord, as I look toward the future with hope,
Help me not to overlook the blessings of today.
Teach me to be grateful for the here and now,
While keeping faith in what's yet to come.
Let gratitude and hope dwell side by side,
As I cherish today and anticipate tomorrow.
May I find joy in both the journey and the dreams,
Balancing contentment with gentle expectation.
Help me to recognize the beauty of this moment,
Even as I trust in the plans You hold for me.
With a grateful heart, may I live each day fully,
Grounded in today and open to tomorrow.
Lord, may gratitude and hope fill my heart,
A light for each step on my journey.

Prayer for Physical Health and Wellness

Prayer for Strength and Energy

Lord, I ask for strength and energy today,
To greet each new beginning with vitality.
Help me to care for the body You've given me,
To nourish it with rest, movement, and care.
May I have the stamina to pursue my purpose,
And the resilience to face challenges ahead.
Grant me energy that sustains and uplifts,
Filling me with the vigour to embrace each day.
Guide me in making choices that support my health,
Honouring the temple of my body as sacred.
Let me recognize the gift of physical strength,
And use it to serve, to grow, and to give.
Lord, bless my body with wellness and vitality,
That I may walk forward with energy and joy.

Prayer for Healing and Renewal

Lord, I ask for healing where it is needed,
That my body may be refreshed and restored.
Help me to release stress and burdens,
And to find peace that renews from within.
May I trust in Your power to heal and restore,
And have faith in my body's ability to renew.
Guide me to choices that foster my wellness,
And to habits that nourish and sustain me.
Let me be patient in my journey to health,
Trusting that healing takes time and grace.
With Your help, may my body feel whole,
Ready to embrace the new with joy and strength.
Lord, bring healing to my body and soul,
Filling me with vitality for each new day.

Prayer for Wellness in Body and Mind

Lord, I seek wellness for my body and mind,
For balance, peace, and strength in all I do.
Help me to care for both my health and spirit,
With choices that bring me closer to wholeness.
Guide me to honour my physical well-being,
And to recognize the connection to my soul.
May I nurture my body with kindness and care,
Seeing wellness as a path to Your light.
Let me move with joy and eat with gratitude,
Resting in the knowledge that I am cared for.
Grant me the clarity to listen to my needs,
And the courage to make choices that serve me.
Lord, bless my journey to health and balance,
So that I may embrace life with peace and vitality.

Prayer for Healthy Habits and Self-Care

Lord, as I embrace new beginnings,
Guide me to form habits that support my health.
Help me to find joy in taking care of my body,
To see self-care as an act of gratitude.
Teach me to rest when I need to,
To nourish myself with mindful choices.
Let exercise and stillness be in harmony,
And may I find balance in all I do.
Grant me discipline and dedication,
To honour my wellness with each choice.
May my habits reflect love for the life You've given,
And my actions show respect for my body.
Lord, let my self-care be a foundation,
A source of strength for all that lies ahead.

Prayer for Health and Gratitude

Lord, I thank You for the gift of my body,
For the strength, energy, and breath within me.
Help me to cherish my health each day,
And to live with gratitude for every moment.
Teach me to appreciate the little things—
The power in my steps, the rhythm of my breath.
May I see health as a blessing, not a given,
And care for myself with humility and love.
Guide me in choices that enhance my wellness,
And lead me away from harm or excess.
Let gratitude be my guide in caring for myself,
Honouring the life and health You've bestowed.
Lord, may my heart be full of thanks,
As I embrace each day with health and joy.

Prayer for Overcoming Doubt and Fear

Prayer for Strength to Face Fear

Lord, when fear threatens to overtake me,
Grant me the strength to stand firm in faith.
Teach me to face the unknown with courage,
Knowing You walk beside me each step of the way.
Help me to remember that fear is fleeting,
But Your love and guidance are constant and true.
When doubts arise, calm my restless mind,
Replacing worry with trust in Your wisdom.
May I find courage not from my own strength alone,
But in the assurance of Your steadfast presence.
Teach me to lean on You when I feel weak,
And to find hope even when the path is unclear.
With each challenge, let my faith grow stronger,
Overcoming fear with love and resilience.
Lord, lead me to confidence rooted in trust,
So that I may walk forward unafraid.

Prayer for Trust in Uncertain Times

Lord, as I journey through unknown paths,
Help me to trust that You are my guide.
In moments when doubt clouds my vision,
Remind me that You hold the way ahead.
Teach me to release the need to control,
And to place my future fully in Your hands.
When I am tempted to worry or fear,
Let Your peace wash over my anxious heart.
May I find courage in Your promises,
Knowing that I am never truly alone.
Strengthen my trust, even in the darkness,
And let me walk by faith, not by sight.
With confidence, I place my steps before You,
Believing You lead me to where I need to be.
Lord, teach me to embrace the unknown with peace,
Trusting in Your divine plan for my life.

Prayer for Confidence in Myself and God

Lord, help me to believe in the strength within,
The gifts You've placed uniquely in my life.
Teach me to trust my abilities and worth,
And to know that I am capable in Your sight.
Let me move forward with self-assurance,
Without fear of failure or self-doubt.
Remind me that You've prepared me for this path,
And that I can rely on both You and myself.
Grant me confidence not rooted in pride,
But in the knowledge that I am held by You.
When challenges come, let my heart not waver,
Trusting in both Your guidance and my strength.
With faith in myself and in Your love,
May I face the future with hope and courage.
Lord, teach me to walk with quiet confidence,
Embracing the fullness of who I am.

Prayer for Peace Amidst Doubt

Lord, when doubt and worry fill my heart,
Grant me the peace to find calm within.
Help me to silence the voices of fear,
And to hear Your reassurance and love.
Teach me that doubt does not define me,
And that fear is a shadow, not my truth.
When I am uncertain about the road ahead,
Let me remember Your faithful promises.
May I find peace in knowing You are near,
Guiding me with patience and grace.
Even in the unknown, let my heart be still,
Finding rest in Your steadfast presence.
With each step, may my doubts diminish,
Replaced by a growing trust in Your plan.
Lord, fill me with peace beyond understanding,
So I may walk forward, untroubled and whole.

Prayer for Boldness in Facing Challenges

Lord, when challenges feel overwhelming,
Give me the boldness to meet them head-on.
Help me to see obstacles as opportunities,
And to overcome fear with faith in You.
Teach me that courage is not the absence of fear,
But the choice to move forward despite it.
Grant me the strength to act with bravery,
Even when I am unsure of what lies ahead.
When I feel small in the face of trials,
Remind me of the power You place within me.
May I rely on Your guidance and my own resolve,
Knowing that together, we are strong.
With boldness, may I embrace each challenge,
Learning and growing through every step.
Lord, let fear be a teacher, not a barrier,
And grant me confidence to keep moving on.

Prayer for Healing After Loss

Prayer for Healing After Loss

Lord, as I step into this new chapter,
Help me to find healing from the pain of loss.
Teach me to carry the memories with love,
But release the weight that holds me back.
May I find peace in knowing You are near,
Comforting me in moments of sorrow.
Guide me through the waves of grief,
And help me rebuild with gentle strength.
Fill my heart with hope for the future,
And remind me that healing takes time.
With Your grace, let me see light again,
A new beginning, though different from before.
Lord, may I find wholeness after this loss,
And embrace life with renewed purpose.

Prayer for Embracing New Beginnings

Lord, in the wake of loss, guide my steps,
As I begin to walk a path of renewal.
Help me to find purpose beyond the grief,
And to seek beauty in each new day.
Teach me to honour the love that was shared,
But to also open my heart to new blessings.
May I find joy in small, gentle moments,
And courage to live fully once again.
Give me strength to rebuild with resilience,
And grace to face the unknown with hope.
Let each step forward be filled with healing,
As I create new memories in this fresh chapter.
Lord, be my guide as I embrace this new life,
And fill my heart with peace and gratitude.

Prayer for Peace Amidst Change

Lord, as I journey through this change,
Grant me peace as I let go of the past.
Help me to hold my memories with love,
While also opening to the promise of tomorrow.
Teach me to be gentle with my heart,
And to allow myself the time to heal.
May peace be my companion in this season,
A quiet strength that carries me onward.
Guide me in finding purpose anew,
Even when the path feels uncertain.
Let peace replace the ache of sorrow,
And hope restore my weary spirit.
Lord, lead me forward with a heart at rest,
Embracing each day with calm and trust.

Prayer for Strength to Move Forward

Lord, in the pain of this loss, grant me strength,
To carry on with hope in my heart.
Teach me to embrace life as it is now,
Honouring what was, but not bound by it.
Help me to live fully, even in sadness,
To find courage in each new step.
Give me strength to rebuild my dreams,
And the faith to trust in brighter days.
Let my sorrow transform into resilience,
A reminder of the love that shaped me.
Guide me to see beyond the grief,
To a future that holds joy once more.
Lord, fill me with strength to keep going,
And to find peace as I create a new path.

Prayer for Finding New Purpose

Lord, in this season of loss, guide my heart,
Helping me to find purpose beyond the pain.
Teach me to see that life still holds meaning,
Even after the sadness of goodbye.
Help me to honour the love that was shared,
And to channel it into acts of kindness.
May I find a new calling in this journey,
A purpose that brings healing and hope.
Lead me toward ways I can make a difference,
Using my experience to uplift and inspire.
Let me find joy in serving others,
A purpose that fills my life once again.
Lord, reveal the path that waits for me,
And help me to live with intention and grace.

Prayer for Comfort and Hope

Lord, in the midst of loss, be my comfort,
A steady presence in times of sorrow.
Help me to see glimpses of hope ahead,
Even when the road feels dark and unknown.
Guide me gently through this season,
Allowing space for both grief and healing.
May I find peace in Your constant love,
A reminder that I am never truly alone.
Let hope be a light that leads me forward,
A quiet assurance that life will bloom again.
With each day, may I feel a bit stronger,
And trust that joy will return in its time.
Lord, bring comfort to my heart and mind,
And lead me into a future filled with peace.

Prayer for Embracing a Fresh Perspective

Prayer for a New Outlook on Challenges

Lord, as I face the challenges before me,
Help me to see them not as barriers but as doors.
Teach me to look beyond the struggle,
And to find the lessons hidden within each trial.
Grant me the wisdom to embrace new perspectives,
To see adversity as a path to growth.
When difficulties arise, strengthen my spirit,
So I may approach them with courage and hope.
Guide me to be resilient and open-minded,
To learn and evolve from every experience.
Let optimism replace doubt in my heart,
And gratitude fill my mind as I journey on.
With each challenge, may I find new strength,
And see Your hand guiding me forward.
Lord, transform my outlook with fresh perspective,
That I may walk in faith and joy each day.

Prayer for Optimism in Every Circumstance

Lord, grant me the gift of optimism,
A heart that looks for light even in darkness.
Teach me to find beauty amidst the struggle,
And to trust that brighter days will come.
Help me to reframe my thoughts with hope,
Seeing possibility where others see limits.
When negativity seeks to cloud my mind,
Let optimism shine as my steady guide.
Fill me with confidence in the future,
Knowing that challenges lead to growth.
Let each day be an opportunity to learn,
And to grow stronger in trust and resilience.
With an optimistic spirit, may I press on,
Seeing every trial as a step toward grace.
Lord, bless my heart with unwavering hope,
And teach me to embrace life with joy.

Prayer for a Mindset Open to Growth

Lord, as I enter this new season,
Grant me a mindset open to change and growth.
Help me to see each challenge as a teacher,
And every hardship as a chance to learn.
Guide me to embrace the unknown with courage,
And to welcome each lesson with an open heart.
May I find strength in times of difficulty,
And seek wisdom in moments of uncertainty.
Teach me to approach life with curiosity,
To explore new perspectives without fear.
Let growth be my focus in all I pursue,
And optimism my companion on this path.
With Your guidance, may I see life anew,
And walk forward with a spirit of adventure.
Lord, help me to welcome change as a blessing,
Trusting that You lead me with purpose and love.

Prayer for Joyful Resilience

Lord, help me to embrace resilience with joy,
To face each setback with a smile and hope.
Teach me to find joy even in challenges,
And to approach trials with a heart of faith.
May I see obstacles as chances to grow,
And difficulties as steps toward strength.
Guide me to be steady, calm, and brave,
Grounded in the belief that all things serve.
Let my spirit be unburdened by worry,
And my heart filled with gratitude and peace.
With optimism as my shield against despair,
May I walk forward in confidence and trust.
Lord, help me to meet life's storms with grace,
And to find joy in the journey, come what may.
Teach me to live with resilient optimism,
Knowing that You walk beside me always.

Prayer for Fresh Eyes and a Grateful Heart

Lord, grant me fresh eyes to see life's beauty,
Even in places I might overlook.
Help me to view each day as a gift,
And to appreciate every moment I am given.
Teach me to let go of past perspectives,
And to embrace each day with a heart renewed.
May I find gratitude in life's simple joys,
And see opportunity in the midst of challenge.
Guide me to approach each moment with wonder,
To notice the blessings that fill my days.
Let optimism fill my heart and mind,
And gratitude lead me in all that I do.
With a fresh perspective, may I live fully,
Embracing the beauty and blessings around me.
Lord, renew my vision and my spirit,
So I may walk in joy and grace each day.

Prayer for Finding Joy in the Journey

Prayer for a New Outlook on Challenges

Lord, as I face the challenges before me,
Help me to see them not as barriers but as doors.
Teach me to look beyond the struggle,
And to find the lessons hidden within each trial.
Grant me the wisdom to embrace new perspectives,
To see adversity as a path to growth.
When difficulties arise, strengthen my spirit,
So I may approach them with courage and hope.
Guide me to be resilient and open-minded,
To learn and evolve from every experience.
Let optimism replace doubt in my heart,
And gratitude fill my mind as I journey on.
With each challenge, may I find new strength,
And see Your hand guiding me forward.
Lord, transform my outlook with fresh perspective,
That I may walk in faith and joy each day.

Prayer for Optimism in Every Circumstance

Lord, grant me the gift of optimism,
A heart that looks for light even in darkness.
Teach me to find beauty amidst the struggle,
And to trust that brighter days will come.
Help me to reframe my thoughts with hope,
Seeing possibility where others see limits.
When negativity seeks to cloud my mind,
Let optimism shine as my steady guide.
Fill me with confidence in the future,
Knowing that challenges lead to growth.
Let each day be an opportunity to learn,
And to grow stronger in trust and resilience.
With an optimistic spirit, may I press on,
Seeing every trial as a step toward grace.
Lord, bless my heart with unwavering hope,
And teach me to embrace life with joy.

Prayer for a Mindset Open to Growth

Lord, as I enter this new season,
Grant me a mindset open to change and growth.
Help me to see each challenge as a teacher,
And every hardship as a chance to learn.
Guide me to embrace the unknown with courage,
And to welcome each lesson with an open heart.
May I find strength in times of difficulty,
And seek wisdom in moments of uncertainty.
Teach me to approach life with curiosity,
To explore new perspectives without fear.
Let growth be my focus in all I pursue,
And optimism my companion on this path.
With Your guidance, may I see life anew,
And walk forward with a spirit of adventure.
Lord, help me to welcome change as a blessing,
Trusting that You lead me with purpose and love.

Prayer for Joyful Resilience

Lord, help me to embrace resilience with joy,
To face each setback with a smile and hope.
Teach me to find joy even in challenges,
And to approach trials with a heart of faith.
May I see obstacles as chances to grow,
And difficulties as steps toward strength.
Guide me to be steady, calm, and brave,
Grounded in the belief that all things serve.
Let my spirit be unburdened by worry,
And my heart filled with gratitude and peace.
With optimism as my shield against despair,
May I walk forward in confidence and trust.
Lord, help me to meet life's storms with grace,
And to find joy in the journey, come what may.
Teach me to live with resilient optimism,
Knowing that You walk beside me always.

Prayer for Fresh Eyes and a Grateful Heart

Lord, grant me fresh eyes to see life's beauty,
Even in places I might overlook.
Help me to view each day as a gift,
And to appreciate every moment I am given.
Teach me to let go of past perspectives,
And to embrace each day with a heart renewed.
May I find gratitude in life's simple joys,
And see opportunity in the midst of challenge.
Guide me to approach each moment with wonder,
To notice the blessings that fill my days.
Let optimism fill my heart and mind,
And gratitude lead me in all that I do.
With a fresh perspective, may I live fully,
Embracing the beauty and blessings around me.
Lord, renew my vision and my spirit,
So I may walk in joy and grace each day.

Disclaimer

Prayers for New Beginnings is intended as a source of inspiration and personal reflection. The prayers and reflections provided in this book are designed to offer spiritual support and encouragement during life's transitions and new chapters. They are not a substitute for professional advice, counselling, or guidance.

Readers are encouraged to seek appropriate professional support for personal, emotional, or psychological issues as needed. The author and publisher are not liable for any outcomes resulting from the use of this book.

This book is inclusive of diverse faith experiences and is written from a non-denominational perspective. It is meant to resonate with individuals from various spiritual backgrounds, with an understanding that each person's journey and relationship with the divine is unique. Readers are encouraged to adapt these prayers to align with their personal beliefs and practices.

Thank you for opening your heart to the journey of new beginnings. May this book serve as a companion of hope and strength as you walk forward into life's unfolding chapters.